THE SCI-FI HAIKU

THE SCI-FI HAIKU

EPOCH 1

Michael Mortenson

For Courtney, Candice, Rebecca, Bayleigh, and
Bryan, who read them first.

CONTENTS

INTRODUCTION

I have a confession to make: I don't read poetry. At least not the push-your-glasses-up-the-bridge-of- your-literary-nose sort of poetry.

What I do read are stories—books of adventure, mystery, humor, and imagination. My challenge in writing this book was to compress these story elements into haiku-sized nuggets.

Some of the haiku in this collection are scientific, some are fictitious, some are stand-alones, and some are related. I'd like to think there are at least seventeen syllables' worth of writing in this collection for everyone. Hopefully many more.

—M.M.

MOONSHOT

According to a video essay I once watched by YouTuber Austin McConnell, the earliest work of science fiction is an ancient Greek novella called *A True Story* by the satirist Lucian of Samosata. It tells the tale of an odyssey to the moon and includes many elements of what we consider science fiction today: mythic heroes, strange alien creatures, interplanetary warfare, and space travel (space travel via cyclone, I might note, which predates Dorothy and her ruby slippers by a good millennium and a half).

True story.

Despite its ancient beginnings, I don't believe science fiction emerged in its modern form until the space race escalated in the sixties. In 1962, US President John F. Kennedy delivered a now-famous speech at Rice University. "We choose to go to the moon," he said, and mainstream contemporary science fiction was born.

Kennedy's moonshot vision, fueled by a rivalry with the Soviet Union, ignited an explosion of innovation in both technology and storytelling, which captured the hearts and imaginations of people across the world. Space travel and the moon landing took center stage in television, film, and pulp paperbacks everywhere.

Since then, rocket ships and space suits have become hallmarks of science fiction. This chapter is a hat tip to anyone who has ever dreamed of going to the moon and to those who have already visited.

SPARK

From the first cave spark
we were destined for the moon,
to walk amongst stars.

INHALATION

That disinfected
lemon, that chrome-filtered air,
that new spaceship smell.

BLAST OFF

Then we're yanked upward.
Gravity roars and spits flame.
At last, we escape.

LAUNCH DAY

Grey plumes arc spaceward.
Daddy says, "Wave to Mommy."
I wave and he cries.

CLAUSTROPHILIA

The suffocating
thrill of knowing the vacuum
of space is waiting.

CAUGHT

No wonder earth has
such love and war—caught we are
'twixt Venus and Mars.

DOWNY SOFT

In space we get by
just fine without mattresses,
snoozing zero-G.

SAGE

A sage master once
told me, "Space is not deadness,"
and I must agree.

ONE SMALL STEP

There, beside my first
footprint, I sign my full name
in shiftless moon dust.

REENTRY

And then I feel hope—
that swelling blue dot fills my
view of space with home.

EMBRACE

I hug her before
she can get her helmet off.
She smells like the moon.

TOUCHDOWN BLUES

What you feel, boots off,
as the last moon dust settles
into the carpet.

ON MISSING

Shoot for the moon and,
if you miss, know that some things
are rocket science.

HARD SCIENCE

Like fine cheeses and drill bits, science fiction stories are often described on a spectrum from hard to soft. On one end of the spectrum, hard science fiction focuses on building stories using scientific knowledge or conjecture, which lends credibility to the story. Think of stories like *Twenty Thousand Leagues Under the Sea* or *The Martian*. Soft science fiction, on the other end of the spectrum, fudges scientific understanding in favor of a cool story. This is the realm of *Star Trek* and *The Time Machine*.

Seen one way, this chapter is my tribute to hard science fiction. The topics covered in these haiku relate to real scientific ideas. So, if you come across an unfamiliar technical topic, don't worry about it. Three minutes on the internet can probably clear up any confusion. Otherwise, use your imagination. The act of making hypotheses—the foundation for much science—is an exercise in imagination.

RECURSIVE

Beginning with the
ending in mind by ending
with the beginning.

ENTROPY

It's not a loss of
energy with age, but a
shift in its nature.

LITANY FOR ALL TIME

Time is the numb-er,
the rift smoother, truth prover,
hurt overcomer.

LAW ONE, NEWTON

When continuing
means casting off the one thing
you can't bear to lose.

LAW TWO, NEWTON

You can't force change, but
as your life accelerates,
you will be forced to.

LAW THREE, NEWTON

They pushed and you pushed
back. For what else could you do?
Physics forced your hand.

THE EVERYTHING SET

The set of all things
must, by a perverse cosmic
joke, contain nothing.

HOOKE'S LAW

If you feel like you've
been forced or displaced, relax,
'cause it all springs back.

FLAT SODA

I warned him, "If you
drink from the Helmholtz bottle,
it will just go flat."

COVALENT BOND

It's funny. The more
we share together, the more
I feel close to you.

IONIC BOND

I'll be your steady
shoulder, your comforter. Go
on now. Hold me close.

METALLIC BOND

Time has a way of
melding us so what is yours
or mine becomes ours.

THE SHAPE OF LOVE

Love's not a cube or
even a tesseract. It's
a Mobius strip.

CAUSTIC BEAUTY

Light through the glass on
my windowsill casts glowing
rings of bright shadow.

REFLECTION

You love a color
not for what it holds, but for
what it reflects back.

KIRCHOFF'S CURRENT LAW

May you never take
more than you can give, nor give
more than you can take.

LIGHTSPEED

Not electric, but
a premonition of speed,
of a breath held back.

CURIOUS STARS

Curious stars in
retrograde motion; in Greek,
wanderers—planets.

SMALL TOWN

I've noticed that sci fi stories about extraterrestrial encounters are often set in small town America. I don't think this is because aliens have a hankering for homemade pies, county fairs, corn fields, or barn dances. No, I think it's people, not aliens, who crave the security, the safety, and the traditional hominess that small towns represent to American audiences.

And why not small-town America? I believe it was good ol' Grandpa Shakespeare who said that the purpose of fiction "was and is, to hold as 'twere the mirror up to nature." In other words, fiction ought to reflect the real world, even as it fabricates a story. If, in the real world, automated agricultural and mining technologies are invading small towns, changing the way things used to be, then isn't a small town the ideal setting for a fictitious story about an invasion from outer space?

The tension between progress and tradition, which is a common theme in sci-fi, comes alive against the backdrop of rusted trucks, porch swings, and fields of wheat. I think of *The Twilight Zone* episode "The Monsters Are Due on Maple Street," which unsettles audiences all the more for its idyllic 1950s small town suburban setting.

This chapter explores these ideas. I envision these haiku finding themselves at home in towns that are little more than a dot on the map—a Mayberry, North Carolina, or Hawkins, Indiana. Places so far away they feel like another planet, but so familiar they smell like home.

FERRIS WHEEL

The Ferris wheel still
spun as the spacecraft beamed us
up into the air.

ABOUT THOSE CIRCLES

Either I'm a sleep-
farming prodigy or them
aliens like corn.

UNABDUCTABLE

They tried beaming up
Ol' Bessie, but that heifer
is solid as bricks.

HEADLINE

Local man survives
home-smashing asteroid thanks
to "brief" outhouse trip.

TICK

I think Joe's ticked off.
He's sick of quantum clock jokes.
Can't get him to tock.

DEAR JANITORIAL

Antigravity
test successful. Sorry for
boot prints on ceiling.

COLLIDE

Confirmed: collider-
made peanut-butter-jelly
molecules exist.

CONSIDERATIONS

Sir, might it be best
not to identify the
said flying object?.

THE OLD BARN

Played moon rangers with
Joe in that old barn. Now a
tree sticks through the roof.

TRUSTY

Super-sonic jet,
fiery dragster, noble steed—
my trusty old bike.

THE SHOE TREE

Lace-tied moon boots slung
high in its boughs—the tree where
old soles go to die.

NOONBERRY

I miss the hammock
in the noonberry tree and
all the winking stars.

ROOFSONG

The cat, my guitar,
our roof and me, strumming thoughts
for the galaxy.

FIREWORKS

We sat on the bench,
I drew her close, and we watched
the meteors blaze.

CUPID

Cupid has rarely
needed his bow since people
started stargazing.

FORTUNE'S SONG

When stars sing bright I
see past yesterday to the
edge of tomorrow.

ROPE BRIDGE

Remember that old
rope bridge at the creek, how the
water shone with moon?

TRACE

I sleep beneath sky,
vast and deep, tracing starpaths
to where you have gone.

PAREIDOLIA

In the moon, in clouds,
in firelit shadows, I see
your face and miss you.

CRYPTID PHOTOGRAPHY

Cryptids, for those unfamiliar with the term, are legendary creatures of conspiracy theory fame—Bigfoot, the Loch Ness monster, and the Yeti, to name a few. My favorite cryptid, though, would have to be the Kraken, the ship-swallowing giant squid.

I picked up Jules Verne's classic sci-fi novel *Twenty Thousand Leagues Under the Sea* in part out of anticipation for the Kraken pictured on the front cover. What I got was mostly a book of extensive lists of fish species and overlong descriptions. Despite the dry parts—pun intended—I finished the story with a greater appreciation for the elements that have shaped science fiction since: the mad adventurer bent on a singular purpose, mysterious sea creatures, and undersea quests.

This haiku series is my take on the ideas in *Twenty Thousand Leagues Under the Sea*. May the spirit of discovery embraced by Verne's novel continue to inspire and capture audiences for many years to come.

PART 1

"Delusion!" they cried.
"You will never photograph
a real, live Kraken."

PART 2

I found a crusty
sub, the *Leaky Sal*, whose name
I hoped was a joke.

PART 3

The *Leaky Sal's* crew
assured me we wouldn't drown.
If I paid them well.

PART 4

We set sail searching
the south seas for the Kraken's
secret resting spot.

PART 5

Six miles off the coast
the sonar readings showed us
a huge biomass.

PART 6

Drawing near, floodlights
revealed a single sightless,
massive, milky eye.

PART 7

Propellers reversed
in stealth mode, we withdrew from
the wide-eyed Kraken.

PART 8

From afar we watched
the sonar map. The Kraken
didn't stir for days.

PART 9

It turns out it's hard
to tell a sleeping Kraken
from one that is dead.

PART 10

Time and cash ran low.
Dead or alive, a Kraken
photo would sell big.

PART 11

One last time we neared
the eye. "Please," I prayed, "don't blink."
My camera flashed.

PART 12

Onboard, I waited,
locked in my makeshift darkroom,
as we sailed shoreward.

PART 13

In horror, I stared
at a high-resolution
picture of my thumb.

A GLINT OF METAL

One of my favorite quotes about computers comes from Pedro Domingos, author of *The Master Algorithm*, a book about machine learning. He said, "People worry that computers will get too smart and take over the world, but the real problem is that they're too stupid and they've already taken over the world." I have to agree. Even the most impressive chess-playing bot is so narrowly specialized that it would struggle to solve a simple algebra problem or write a sentence. But that doesn't stop science fiction writers from pretending computers are capable of anything.

Science fiction stories like to imagine a world without the limitations of current technology. What if, in the future, the line grows blurry between a body and a machine, a brain and a computer, a soul and a program? This is the primary science fiction tension of Mary Shelley's *Frankenstein*—humans grappling with the consequences of pushing the limits of science and technology.

Aligned with this tradition, I give you a Franken-chapter of sorts, exploring what happens at the interface between the living and the technological. Welcome to a world of robots and machines: humorous, horrific, eerie, or endearing. The future awaits.

GLINT

The wolf paced, watching,
steps hinged, and behind its eyes
a glint of metal.

SILVER

A circuit board of
silver veins feeds the heart of
the ironwood tree.

IRONWOOD

The windstorm flared and
the whole ironwood forest
shivered, creaked, and clanged.

CRICKETS

The tree thrummed with one
thousand mechanized crickets.
Then, as one, they launched.

GHOST TALK

Vines on steel girders,
wind past taxicab tailpipes—
ghost metropolis.

FAN

Two boxing robots
streamed from a still stadium
to thousands of fans.

SPARKFLINT

Since the sky went dark,
we've lived by electric light.
It's time we made fire.

STUCK

Since tomorrow I've
been fixing the time machine.
Just like yesterday.

RAVEN

Don't cross Peg-leg Bart
and his watch-raven with the
mechanical eye.

PILOT OF THE OLD GUARD

Legend says he's spent
so long with mechs, he rusts and
drinks petroleum.

PILOT'S OATH

Once inside, I am
not my own. I am the dread
ghost in the machine.

THE FINAL BLOW

"Buck up, kid," they said,
"Your mech did it, not you." Still,
at night, his fist rang.

CONTROL

The mech stopped fighting,
turned, and marched on the city.
With me, trapped inside.

KNOT

Never nod off in
the care of a prototype
hairstyling robot.

CHATBOT

The well-trained chatbot
knows, when wooing, it's best to
use a cursive font.

LOOP

I leave myself notes,
but I wish they had made me
with more memory.

GIFT

The gift, a rose, was
holographic, but the flush
of her cheeks was real.

FIRST DATE

This girl was a dream.
But when her hand passed straight through
mine, dream turned to dread.

WEARING CAPES

I love superhero stories as much as the next guy. Give me that daring figure in a mask and cape, hordes of mutant monsters, cackling villains, physics-defying powers, and crisp action sequences. While superhero stories borrow from many genres, I believe that without science fiction's contribution—from radioactive spiders to alien saviors with sensitivities to glowing minerals—the superhero genre would never have left the ground.

Beneath the exaggerated physiques, mustache twirling, and fisticuffs, I believe superhero stories represent a response to something deeply human—helplessness. Each day people are pummeled with terrifying news stories they are powerless to do anything about: war, crime, social upheaval, political scandal, poverty, and natural disasters, to name a handful. In an age of information, superheroes let us believe, for a moment, in a good-versus-evil world where individuals can make a difference.

I've heard people decry the superhero genre for glorifying violence, stereotyping, or pushing body ideals, and although many of those accusations carry merit, the genre still relentlessly claims new fans each year. Why? Because, in a world helplessly drowning in information, I believe there are those who hope, if secretly, to be rescued.

These haiku go out to the storytellers who help us hope for heroes in our midst.

GET RICH QUICK

The best business in
a superhero city
is window repair.

LUNCH

Sure, I've puked on my
cape, but sometimes it's my lunch
or the greater good.

LASER VISION

Laser vision has
many uses. For instance,
I can read barcodes.

KICKS

I stepped in sludge. Now
my shoes walk up walls, so I
keep my laces tight.

SUBTLE

I prefer subtle
villainy. One sock, gone in
the wash. Yeah, that's me.

FLIGHT

Looking back, my real
power wasn't flight; it was
helping others fly.

LATE

What's my name? Slothman.
If I'm your hero, you know
you've had a long day.

PERKS

With great power comes
great responsibility
and . . . a cape discount?

HELICOPTER PARENTS

I wish they were just
helicopter parents. It's
a bit much with drones.

I BROUGHT A STICK

The drums boomed. The crowd
cheered. The beast rattled its cage.
Sure, I thought, *fair fight*.

USB

Fine. Laugh. But could you
plug in the kill code flash drive
right on the first try?

THWARTED

That moment you stop
your monologue 'cause they laced
lunch with laxatives.

HEADQUARTERS

Island ringed by toothed
rocks, accessible only
by motor-surfboard.

A SIMPLE PLOT

Last, we'll swap labels
for their Deploy Warheads and
Self-Destruct buttons.

STRANGE BEASTS

Kaiju is a Japanese word which translates to "strange beast" in English. The term is used to refer to a subgenre of films popularized in Japan about gargantuan, city-ravaging monsters. Think *Godzilla*.

My first kaiju movie was *Pacific Rim*, which a friend convinced me to watch. The movie was a solid action movie as far as I was concerned, but it mostly felt designed to gratify a certain brand of primal bloodlust via epic gladiatorial monster-vs-robot battles. However, as I later looked into the film genre's origin, I uncovered a sobering history hidden beneath the veneer of blockbuster action.

The genre came into being in the aftermath of World War II. Especially in early kaiju films, the metropolis-flattening monsters can be seen as fictional stand-ins for the very real atomic bomb dropped on Nagasaki in August of 1945 by U.S. armed forces.

Today, our kaiju might represent any number of devastating natural disasters or military conflicts, and it is not uncommon for kaiju-like monsters to feature in sister genres within science fiction. For example, many superhero movies include a kaiju battle at some point near the climax. In my mind, kaiju films are the Japanese twin of American superhero films, since both feature forces beyond people's control. I suspect my friend loves kaiju movies for the way they show the resiliency and resourcefulness of comparatively ordinary humans.

For many, kaiju movies remain a glorious escape into slow-motion action with oversized monsters. For me, the kaiju subgenre represents a challenge to explore what it means to live in a world with massive monsters through a miniature window the size of a haiku.

ORIGINS

Tame and curious,
young kaiju lost in death, cries.
Flame and furious.

SKYWRITTEN

They say some read clouds—
whispers of storms behind or
volcanoes ahead.

AWAKENED

Ocean, flat as glass,
shattered by surging mountain
with green eyes and fangs.

THAW

Ice-fringed behemoth
stops at local volcano
to thaw aching wings.

MONSTER TEETH

Try hand-carved dentures!
Two thousand made from just one
harvested molar.

KAIJU MENU

The tang of tarmac,
crunch of glass, fresh steel rebar:
all acquired tastes.

WARNING

The monster siren
wasn't fixed yet, but we heard
it coming just fine.

FOOTPRINT

Despite the concrete,
diving board, and splashing kids,
it's still a footprint.

DESSERT

To a kaiju, a

T-Rex looks like a cupcake.

We look like sprinkles.

VERSUS

Mechatronic fists
are no match for rust-breathing,
hammerhead dragons.

EXTINCT

Biologists should
not say this, but sometimes I'm
glad things go extinct.

HOT-WIRING SPACESHIPS

One of the most popular subgenres of science fiction is space opera. Space operas are adventure stories that often feature intergalactic wars, spaceship battles, swashbuckling heroes, and daring quests. The Star Wars franchise is probably the most well-known example of space opera, although the modern tradition traces back to Edgar Rice Boroughs' John Carter of Mars books.

Space operas, especially in film, share significant DNA with westerns. This is how you get saloons, wanted posters, bounty hunters, and quickdraw standoffs in Star Wars shows. I once heard John Carter described as an action hero with the voice of a Southern gentleman.

No collection of science fiction haiku would be complete without acknowledging the tremendous impact space opera has had on the genre. So, here's to bandits and smugglers, to heroes and villains, to quests across the galaxy— to adventure in space.

SKILLS

If only I knew
a keycode or spark trick to
hot-wire a spaceship.

THE PROSPECTOR

Spits sunflower seeds
and pans the asteroid belt—
he ain't struck gold yet.

FRIDGE NOTE

Mom—Sorry I skipped
town. Moon flower is yours. Love,
Sam the Space Bandit

SUPERNOVA SURFER

Stardust sprays behind
her board as she carves a path
between nebulae.

CRACKS

She broke our hatch seal
on accident. I yelled. Now,
I'm left patching cracks.

PRESSURE

I eyed the cracked hull,
set course for earth, and prayed to
the god of duct tape.

PUSH

Taking a deep breath,
I pushed off the space station
trusting my tether.

TENTACLES

"Come, let me hold you,"
it said, tentacles squirming.
I gripped my blaster.

THE START

The two astronauts
held hands and leaned in slowly
till their helmets touched.

SINATRA

He dimmed the cabin,
Sinatra over the comms,
and slow danced mid-air.

IN TRANSIT

Had them beam a box
of chocolates from base for you.
Sorry they melted.

FUZZY

Don't forget to pack
null-G magnetic litter
for your pet space cat.

LIGHT SWORDS

We call them light swords
for the keen laser blade, Ma'am,
not for the low weight.

HELMET

What makes smart-helmets
so smart? Well, you see, stupid
people don't wear them.

SUIT

Suits keep your insides
inside, so I don't care if
you think you look fat.

LEAK

If nature calls, hang
up. We can't afford to break
biocontainment.

CRISPY

Jet rotisserie
comes in two tasty flavors:
crispy char and burnt.

SOUR

"Enough?" my Martian
host asked. I grimaced at the
sour soup. "More, she wants!"

AN ALIEN FEAR

The fear is not our
loneliness, but that they, too,
are lonely creatures.

UNFORM

Few live long enough
to witness how sky-patterns
unform. But I have.

BRING ME THE MOON

Bring me the moon, Son,
and this time, don't spill the light.
I want my moon full.

CRYSTAL

Pathfinder crystals
will guide you true, but your path
may be the long one.

EACH BEAUTY

I shouldn't be shocked
each planet has beauty, but
each does, and I am.

SPROUT

I cried, watering
red soil with tears, when I saw
the first leaf on Mars.

BLOOMS

Once a forgotten
sunflower seed on red Mars.
Now a yellow sea.

ROOF

Rain pings off panels,
scavenged from spaceship wreckage.
Rooftop lullaby.

ICE CAVE

Pockmarked ice cave walls
bright with frozen phosphocytes
trapped, but still glowing.

CEASELESS

Still the center stirs,
shifting gentle and ceaseless
as lunar tidelines.

MOONSONG

Sing to the twin moons,
to the high moon, to the low,
a song of silver.

A SONG
ON SOLAR WIND

As far as I can tell, the main difference between poetry and prose is form. Prose is built with sentences, paragraphs, and chapters, while poetry is built with lines, stanzas, and word-level constraints. For example, haiku poems in the Japanese tradition are 17 syllables long, split into lines with a 5-7-5 syllable pattern. Haiku purists would add that haiku poetry ought to focus on themes of nature while including a *kigo*, or seasonal reference, and a *kireji*, or "cutting word," usually at the end. So, most of the poems in this book are not traditional haiku.

Some might classify the poems in this book as *senryu,* which are essentially haiku about people instead of nature. But many sci-fi haiku aren't even senryu. (Do robots count as people?) I think most sci-fi haiku share more material with micro-fiction, like the six-word story, than senryu. However you choose to classify the poems in this book, I hope you've discovered at least seventeen syllables that will follow you home.

This final chapter is a serialized sci-fi story in haiku-sized chapters. It was inspired by a cricket hiding in the grass one summer afternoon, which is as haiku-y an inspiration as you'll find.

LOG ENTRY 2313

Touched down. Violent storm
on atmospheric entry.
System report: wet.

LOG ENTRY 2315

Bivouac deployed.

Transport in need of repair.

Will likely take weeks.

LOG ENTRY 2316

Found crag not far from
camp overlooking a sea
of space-algae green.

LOG ENTRY 2318

Scan says air level
safe, but I'm still afraid to
take off my helmet.

LOG ENTRY 2321

May abandon plan
to repair transport. Repair
transponder instead?

LOG ENTRY 2322

Found out today what
air tasted like back before
refabrication.

LOG ENTRY 2327

At the crag by the
sea, removed helmet and heard
a day cricket sing.

LOG ENTRY 2328

Brine cell needs refill.
Transponder won't work unless
I find a bucket.

LOG ENTRY 2329

Broke protocol to
ferry green sea brine to ship
with my own helmet.

LOG ENTRY 2330

Transponder fixed. Sent
signal, but hesitated.
Will miss day crickets.

LOG ENTRY 2339

Mission control says
I should have died. The truth? My
crash taught me to live.

LOG ENTRY 2348

I watched the planet's
green seas fade away from view.
Farewell, Verdera.

LOG ENTRY 2352

Cricket chirps nonstop—
a song on solar wind. Ship
captain's peeved. I smile.

REFERENCES

Harvey, Ryan. "A History of Godzilla on Film, Part 1: Origins (1954–1962)." blackgate.com. Wordpress, December 16, 2013. blackgate.com/2013/12/16/a- history-of-godzilla-on-film-part-1-origins-1954-1962.

Kennedy, John F. "Address at Rice University on the Nation's Space Effort." jfklibrary.org. John F. Kennedy Presidential Library and Museum. Accessed October 24, 2022. jfklibrary.org/learn/about- jfk/historic-speeches/address-at-rice-university-on- the-nations-space-effort.

Langston, Jennifer. "A Q&A With Pedro Domingos: Author of 'The Master Algorithm'." washington. edu. University of Washington News, September 17, 2015. washington.edu/news/2015/09/17/a-q-a-with- pedro-domingos-author-of-the-master-algorithm.

McConnell, Austin. "The Absurd 2nd Century Space Opera You'll Never Read." YouTube, 2022. youtube.com/watch?v=UBpDdlirzH0.

Shakespeare, William. *The Tragedy of Hamlet, Prince of Denmark*. gutenberg.org. Project Gutenberg, November 1998. gutenberg.org/files/1524/1524-h/1524-h.htm.

HOW TO SUPPORT AUTHORS

All authors, whether traditionally published or self-published, are technically small business owners. Of course, we authors would like to spend as much of our time writing as possible, but the reality is that most of us spend a great deal of time on non-writing tasks like marketing and book promotion (and maybe working a second job to pay the rent.)

People want to know how to support their favorite authors, but often don't know what to do. The first and most obvious way to show support is by buying books. However, if you really want to support an author, buy their book and then gift them more time to write by doing a little marketing and book promotion. Leave a review online. Share on social media. Recommend the book to a friend. Make some fan art.

I think I speak for all authors when I say thank you for reading. Your support and trust in us mean the world. If you would like to stay up to date with all things sci-fi haiku, you can follow @thescifihaiku on Instagram. Finally, if you'll indulge my flattery for a moment, allow me to say, reading looks good on you. Keep it up!

ABOUT THE AUTHOR

Michael Mortenson is an author, poet, and essayist from Las Vegas, Nevada. His debut poetry collection *The Sci-fi Haiku* won the 2022 LDSPMA Emerging Author Award in poetry. Mortenson holds a master's degree in physics, and his work often blends the technical with the creative. If you enjoy his work, you can follow @thescifihaiku on Instagram.

* 9 7 9 8 9 8 7 4 3 1 7 0 2 *